WILD RECEIVER

by HOSS MASTERSON   illustrated by JOSH ALVES

STONE ARCH BOOKS
a capstone imprint

is published by Stone Arch Books,
A Capstone Imprint
1710 Roe Crest Drive
North Mankato, Minnesota 56003
www.mycapstone.com

Cataloging in Publication information is available at the Library of Congress website.

ISBN: 978-1-4965-4307-3 (hardcover)
ISBN: 978-1-4965-4311-0 (paperback)
ISBN: 978-1-4965-4323-3 (eBook PDF)

Summary: Bobby Longbeak is a very talented football turkey but needs to learn to keep his wild streak under control.

Illustrator: Josh Alves
Editor: Nate LeBoutillier
Designer: Kristi Carlson

Printed and bound in the USA.
010008S17

TABLE OF CONTENTS

MVPS

BOBBY LONGBEAK
The star "wild" receiver of the Turkeys has touchdown talent.

OCHO UNO
This good friend and mentor to Bobby Longbeak used to be a trash-talking turkey.

ARISTOTLE SCREECH-EYE
The intimidating Owls linebacker is both tough and smart.

CHAPTER ONE

THROW IT TO BOBBY LONGBEAK

Late in the fourth quarter, the Turkeys trailed the Bobcats, 28-23. It was third down. The Turkeys needed 16 yards for the first down.

The Turkeys huddled up. Johnny Wattle was not happy. And when the quarterback wasn't happy, nobody was happy. "Get your hind quarters in gear and block!" he yelled.

Wide receiver Bobby Longbeak flapped his wing at Wattle. He said, "Wattle, you just get the ball to Bobby Longbeak."

Bobby Longbeak's name was always in the newspaper or on the Internet. His name was always on TV and radio. Reporters repeated it all the time.

BOBBY LONGBEAK MAKES A BEAUTIFUL CATCH!

BOBBY LONGBEAK SCORES THE TOUCHDOWN!

BOBBY LONGBEAK DANCES THE MOONCLAW IN THE END ZONE!

Bobby Longbeak heard his own name over and over. He heard it so often that he stopped thinking of himself as *me* and started thinking of himself as *Bobby Longbeak*. So he stopped calling himself *me* and called himself Bobby Longbeak like everyone else did.

"Come on, Wattle," said Bobby Longbeak. "If you throw it to Bobby Longbeak, Bobby Longbeak is going to catch it."

Some of the other Turkeys gobbled under their breath. They were tired of Bobby Longbeak showing off. They were tired of him talking about money or fame or himself. They were a team. Bobby Longbeak was selfish.

Wattle said to Longbeak, "If you're open, I'll throw you the ball. If not, I'll hit some other Turkey." He called a play and clapped his wings. The Turkeys broke their huddle.

Bobby Longbeak lined up wide left, near the Bobcat sideline. Longbeak started jerking his neck back and forth, faster and faster. He had a dollar sign braided into his turkey beard. It waved in the breeze.

Johnny Wattle got ready. He gobbled out signals. "Omaha! Omaha!"

The center snapped the ball. The players crashed together. Gobbling and yowling echoed in the stadium. Fur flew. Feathers floated.

Wattle rolled left. He saw Longbeak running free. Wattle fired. Bobby Longbeak dove and brought in the ball with one wing. He got two claws down inbounds.

FIRST DOWN!

Bobby Longbeak twirled the ball on the ground. He sprinted up and down the Bobcat sideline. Fat felines hissed and snarled. A cat in a headset waved a clipboard and arched his back.

The official took his whistle out of his mouth. "Calm down, Longbeak," he said. "I'll throw a penalty flag."

"But I'm Bobby Longbeak," said Bobby Longbeak. "I'm the best in the league. You can't flag me!"

"I can, and I will," said the official. "Quit flapping your feathers."

The Turkeys ran the ball. The clock stopped at the two-minute warning.

During the timeout, Longbeak told Wattle, "Get the ball to Bobby Longbeak. Bobby Longbeak wants to go deep."

Johnny Wattle smoothed his feathers. "Don't be a snood," he said. "Just get open. We'll see what happens."

The official blew his whistle. The play clock began to tick.

Turkeys and Bobcats lined up. Wattle moved under center. The center snapped the ball. Wattle dropped back to pass. He saw Longbeak. The QB heaved the ball just before he got tackled.

The ball was long, but not too long for Bobby Longbeak. Longbeak sped up. He made an over-the-beak catch and marched into the endzone. roared the announcer.

Touchdown for Bobby Longbeak!

The crowd chanted his name.

Bob-by Long-beak!

Bob-by Long-beak!!

BOBBY LONGBEAK!!!

Bobby Longbeak spiked the ball. Then he gobbled. Then he flapped his wings. Then he danced. While doing the Moonclaw, he bumped into Junior Meow.

Junior Meow was the toughest linebacker around. "Longbeak!" he said. "I'm coming for you!"

Longbeak jerked his neck back and forth. He flapped his wings and side-stepped.

The official threw a yellow flag. "Personal foul. Offense, Number 84. Excessive celebration. Fifteen yards to be assessed on the kick."

Wattle smacked Longbeak's helmet. "Knock it off," Wattle said. "Get over to the bench and be quiet."

The Turkeys went for the two-point conversion, but the try failed. Junior Meow was extra mad after Longbeak's dancing. He stuffed the play. The Turkeys led by a single point, 29-28.

The kicking units came on. Normally, the Turkeys would kick from their own 35-yard line. Because of Longbeak's penalty, they were moved back to the 20.

The kick . . . *A BOOMER!*

But the return . . . *LOOK OUT!*

A Bobcat player caught the ball and ran all the way past midfield. The Bobcats were already in field goal range.

After a few more plays, the Bobcat kicker trotted onto the field. One snap, one hold, and one perfect kick followed.

The Bobcats won, 31-29. Bobby Longbeak and the Turkeys lost.

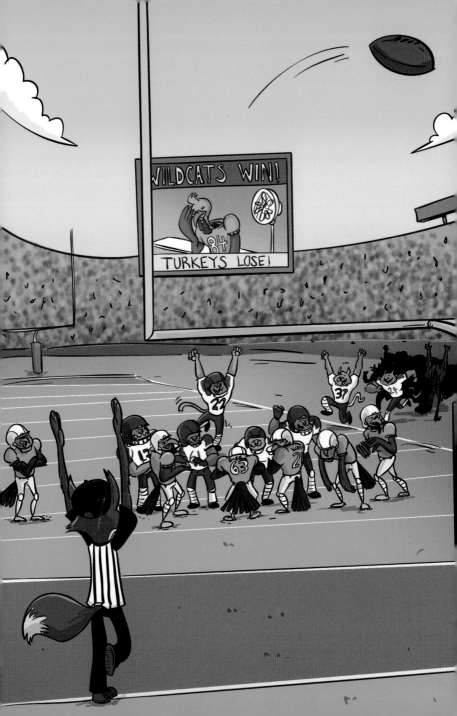

CHAPTER TWO

A CLASSY TURKEY

It was the postgame news conference. Who do you suppose Bobby Longbeak talked about? That's right. He talked about himself. Good old Bobby Longbeak.

Reporters gathered around to get the scoop. Sometimes Bobby Longbeak would say crazy things. They liked to hear him talk. And Bobby Longbeak had no problem gobbling.

A honker from the *Goose Gazette* asked if Longbeak had any regrets.

Longbeak said no.

A woodchuck from the *Daily Chip* noted that Longbeak's penalty set up the Bobcats' winning field goal.

Longbeak blamed the defense. In fact, he always blamed the defense. Not once had Bobby Longbeak taken the blame.

A possum from the *Sleepy Eye Post* asked if he would prepare differently for next week.

"Next week," said Longbeak, "I'll be better than ever. If that's even possible. "

Once the press left, Bobby Longbeak sat alone in front of his locker. His coolness melted. He knew he'd let his team down. His penalty for overdoing it in the end zone made it easier for the Bobcats to win. Bobby Longbeak felt guilty.

The receiver got his phone out of his locker. He looked through his contacts and hit up Ocho Uno. An old Turkey wide receiver, Ocho Uno was now retired. Ocho Uno and Bobby Longbeak had been tight since they were young. They made plans to meet at the Fallen Oak restaurant.

* * *

Ocho Uno sat at a fancy table at the Fallen Oak. Animals around him dined on fine acorns and wild grapes. Ocho Uno was a classy turkey, but it hadn't always been that way.

Ocho Uno used to be a loudmouth. He used to prance, dance, and boast. He used to be a lot like the turkey who sat across the table from him: Bobby Longbeak.

The doe waiting tables at the Fallen Oak dropped off a tray. It was full of plump worms and slugs. The doe returned with two glasses of muddy water.

Ocho Uno pointed at the water. "It's Missouri River water," he said. "It's fantastic."

Longbeak sipped and savored. It was indeed fine water. He said, "I've been Bobby Longbeakin' again."

Ocho Uno said, "I don't want to hear about anymore Bobby Longbeakin'. You be quiet, now. Just listen."

Longbeak slurped down a slug. He sipped his Missouri River water.

Ocho Uno said, "You can't disrespect defenders like that."

"Look who's talking," said Longbeak.

"I said be quiet. Just listen." Ocho Uno stroked his beard. "They don't need that kind of dancing and jumping around. It's ridiculous."

Bobby Longbeak smiled.

"I'm not kidding," said Ocho Uno. "When you're done playing ball, do you want folks to remember you?"

"They already know my name," he said.

"They may know your name, but do they really know *you*?" Ocho Uno asked.

"What in the forest are you talking about?" Longbeak said.

"Do you know how many animals know my name?" Ocho asked.

"Everyone in beast mode knows your name!" said Longbeak. "You are a legend!"

Ocho Uno took off his shades. "They know me as Ocho Uno," he said. "But how many know my real name? Do *you* even know my real name?"

"It's . . . " Longbeak stopped. "Brad or Chad or something? Right?"

"See?" said Ocho Uno. "No one knows. They know me as the turkey who screwed around. Number Eighty-One. Ocho Uno."

"But," said Longbeak, jutting his neck back and forth, "I'm Bobby Longbeak."

"That won't mean much for long," said Ocho Uno. "Not with that attitude. Quit showing off. Quit bragging. And quit blaming everyone else."

Bobby Longbeak looked around. Animals were enjoying their dinners at the Fallen Oak. He wished he could just enjoy his. But something was bothering him.

CHAPTER THREE

EJECTED!

Bobby Longbeak woke up early the next morning. He went for a trot along the river. Mist hung over the water. The rising sun cast shadows in the trees. He jogged through the mud.

Another jogger ran toward him. The jogger appeared to be a bobcat. A big one. It was the Bobcats' linebacker, Junior Meow — the cat Bobby Longbeak had bumped into during his touchdown dance. The big linebacker came to a stop. Meow growled. "Longbeak!"

Bobby Longbeak stopped running and faced the bobcat. He wanted more than anything to dance and jump around. He wanted to put on his normal act that showed folks he was Bobby Longbeak — a confident, strong, and talented turkey. Instead, Bobby Longbeak said, "Do you know Ocho Uno's real name?"

Junior Meow shrugged his shoulders. He said, "Ocho Uno's real name? I have no idea."

"That's what I thought," Bobby Longbeak said. He began to jog again.

The linebacker stood there and snarled.

* * *

On Sunday, the Turkeys squared off against the New Bark Beavers. They were big, fat rodents and could muscle even wolves off the line of scrimmage. They had a hot-headed linebacker of their own, Clarence Tailer. The Turkeys expected a physical game.

The Beavers kicked the ball out of the end zone. The Turkeys started from the 20-yard line.

In the huddle, quarterback Johnny Wattle said, "Longbeak, look. They'll try to bump you at the line. Shake past and go deep. I want an 80-yard bomb, right now."

The Turkeys set up on the line. Wattle called the signals, gobbling: "Omaha! Omaha!" The center snapped the ball. Wattle dropped back.

The Beaver linebacker, Clarence Tailer, let Longbeak take one step. He shoved him in the chest. Longbeak stumbled. Then Clarence Tailer bumped him again. Longbeak spun away.

Longbeak streaked down the sideline. He turned on the speed. Wattle threw as far as he could. The ball sailed. Longbeak slowed down just a tad, but it was enough for Clarence Tailer to catch up. The big beaver brought his powerful tail down on Longbeak's back. Longbeak went flying to the ground before the ball arrived.

The ball landed. The official threw a yellow flag. Clarence Tailer had made contact too early.

"Pass interference, defense," said the official.

The Turkeys got the ball at midfield. They tried a couple of runs, but the Beavers stopped them. It was third and long.

In the huddle, Johnny Wattle looked at Bobby Longbeak. He said, "Longbeak, go inside this time. You can burn them all day. You got this!"

The center snapped the ball. Wattle dropped back. Again, the Beaver cornerback nailed Longbeak in the chest. Longbeak staggered and broke to the inside.

Wattle was under pressure. He side-winged the ball at Longbeak, who was slanting across the field.

Clarence Tailer hauled off and delivered a shoulder blow to Longbeak's head. Tailer hit Longbeak right on the dollar sign. Longbeak could not hold on to the pass.

Longbeak felt dizzy. As he stood, he saw Tailer arguing with the official, who had thrown another flag, this time for targeting. Tailer left the referee to taunt Longbeak.

"Longbeak!" said the linebacker. "You're more chicken than turkey."

Longbeak started flapping his wings and gobbling. He was about to start dancing when Clarence Tailer clobbered him.

It took a second for Bobby Longbeak's world to stop spinning. But when he got to his feet, he realized that he and Clarence Tailer had been ejected. The referees had thrown both players right out of the game.

CHAPTER FOUR

THE REAL BOBBY LONGBEAK

All the teams in the Forest Conference have hot tubs in their locker rooms. After he got ejected, Bobby Longbeak retreated to the locker room and climbed in the hot tub. The water was perfect, mucky as a creek bed. He laid his head against the side. He thought, *What have I done?*

The Turkeys lost, 24-17. If Longbeak hadn't lost his cool, the Turkeys could have won. Once again he had let his team down.

Longbeak took a long time getting dressed. He went to the postgame press conference.

An old duck from the *Green Lagoon Tribune* asked, "Bobby, can you dance for us? We didn't get to see the Moonclaw in the game."

Longbeak shook his head. The reporters thought he was being funny. They laughed.

A coyote from the *Woodland Examiner* asked, "Who would win in a dance-off? You or Ocho Uno?"

Longbeak rolled his beady eyes.

A squirrel from *TREE-S-P-N Sports* said, "Next week, will Bobby Longbeak be Bobby Longbeak?"

Longbeak walked out of the press conference.

The desire to be alone led Bobby Longbeak to the river. He strutted along the muddy bank and plopped down in some weeds. His phone was blowing up. There were calls and texts from Ocho Uno, Johnny Wattle, and reps from the Forest Conference. They all wanted to know what his problem was. Why had he acted so rude at the press conference?

He had lost his temper during the game as well as after. Now, he was mad for having gotten mad. Why was that? Because he was being the fake Bobby Longbeak.

He listened to the water, its calm flow and light slapping against the banks. He said, "It's time to be the real Bobby Longbeak."

CHAPTER FIVE

A NEW TURKEY

Next Sunday, the Game of the Week was the Turkeys versus the Barn Owls. The scouting reports were out. You could beat the Turkeys if you got inside Longbeak's head. Everyone knew it.

The Barn Owls had the perfect player to do it: the Professor of Defense himself, strong safety Aristotle Screech-Eye.

Owls are smart birds, and Screech-Eye was the smartest of the smart. After he made a tackle, he tried to scare opponents with knowledge. He would ask the ball carrier to solve a tough math problem or name a state's capital. If the player couldn't do it in, like, two seconds, he would pound his chest and yell, "You fail!"

If that wasn't bad enough, he looked fierce. He wore shaded goggles with flames painted on the sides. Some of Screech-Eye's opponents saw him in their bad dreams.

Everyone in the woods thought Longbeak would lose his mind. And they thought that Screech-Eye would be the one to make him do it.

If the Turkeys lost three in a row? Well, their playoff hopes would be ruined.

Ocho Uno was at the game. He found Longbeak during warm-ups and said, "I'll be up in the luxury box. I don't want to see anymore crazy Longbeakin'."

Longbeak said, "You won't. I'm a new turkey."

"Hey!" said Ocho Uno. "You didn't call yourself Bobby Longbeak."

"Those days are over," Longbeak said.

"That's more like it! I want to see a wide receiver. You hear me? If I see a *wild* receiver, I'll slap you silly."

Longbeak laughed. The two friends wing-bumped. Ocho Uno headed up to the luxury box.

The Turkeys took possession at their own 20-yard line. Coming out of the huddle, Bobby Longbeak heard Screech-Eye hooting.

"Hey, Longbeak!" said the Professor of Defense. "You're zero minus one. You're less than nothing. You're gonna fail."

Quarterback Johnny Wattle came up under center. He gobbled out signals. "Omaha! Omaha!" Wattle dropped back to pass.

The Owl corner dropped into a zone, forcing Longbeak into Screech-Eye's territory. Wattle faked. Screech-Eye fell for it. Longbeak cut back up the field. Wattle heaved the ball . . .

LONGBEAK WITH THE CATCH!

HE!

COULD!

GO!

ALL!

THE!

WAY!

When Longbeak broke the plane of the goal line, he raised his wing. He wanted to dance. He wanted to spike the ball. But he gathered himself and simply tossed it over to the official.

The referee caught the ball and smiled. He said, "Atta boy, Longbeak."

Longbeak trotted like a regular turkey back to his sideline. The Professor of Defense ran up and got all up in Longbeak's feathers. "What's the capitol of North Dakota?" he screamed.

Longbeak smiled.

Screech-Eye hooted, "What's 27 times 450?"

Longbeak turned away.

Screech-Eye was getting frantic. "Why does the moon pull the tides? How many yards equal a foot? What came first — the chicken or the egg?"

Bobby Longbeak went to the sideline and sat on the bench. He took a swig of Featherade.

A coach with a headset came up. He said to Longbeak, "It's Ocho Uno. He wants to talk." The coach placed the headset on Longbeak's head.

"Longbeak!" Ocho Uno said. "There is hope for you yet!"

Longbeak swallowed a gobble. He'd have to treat his friend to some slugs at the Fallen Oak. They'd do a toast. To the new Bobby Longbeak!

And the new Bobby Longbeak did something unlike the old Bobby Longbeak. He kept his beak shut for the rest of the game.

ABOUT THE AUTHOR

Born on the range in Montana and raised partly by wolves (just kidding, unless you count his three big brothers), Hoss Masterson is no stranger to living the life wild. By trade, he's been a hired farmhand, a sportswriter, a teacher, and a musician (bass guitar and harmonica). He enjoys old Westerns, birdwatching, cropchecking, and a good yarn.

ABOUT THE ILLUSTRATOR

International award-winning illustrator Josh Alves loves creating art and visiting schools to encourage creativity. He lives in Maine with his incredible wife and their four clever kids. Learn more about him at www.joshalves.com.

GLOSSARY

cornerback (KOR-nur-bak) – player on defense who often guards a wide receiver

penalty (PEN-uhl-tee) – punishment for breaking a rule

linebacker (LINE-bak-uhr) – player on defense who is very big and athletic and usually makes the most tackles

quarterback (KWAR-turh-bak) – player who leads the offense and often passes the ball

snood (SNOOD) – a wrinkled fold of skin that hangs over a turkey's beak

taunting (TAWNT-ing) – to mock or tease in an insulting way

touchdown (TUHCH-down) – the play where a player carries the football over the goal line and scores six points

wide receiver (WIDE re-SEEV-uhr) – player on offense who catches the quarterback's passes

TALK ABOUT IT!

1. Why did Bobby Longbeak like to dance and celebrate?

2. How did losing and being ejected affect Bobby Longbeat?

3. Why did Bobby Longbeak ignore Aristotle Screech-Eye?

WRITE ABOUT IT!

1. Write a list of the things you'd like to be remembered for someday.

2. What if Bobby Longbeak was a rapper? Write some rhymes that he might use.

3. Write a short story about Aristotle Screech-Eye's childhood as a young owl.

WILD TURKEY FACTS

 can change the color of their heads when excited from red to pink and even blue

 able to run up to 25 miles per hour

 consist of five different species

 when in a group, can be called a crop, dole, gang, posse, or a raffle

 chosen by Benjamin Franklin to be the United States' national bird but was beaten out by the bald eagle

 sport between 5,000 and 6,000 feathers.

THE FUN DOESN'T STOP HERE!

DISCOVER MORE AT WWW.CAPSTONEKIDS.COM

VIDEOS & CONTESTS • GAMES & PUZZLES
FRIENDS & FAVORITES • AUTHORS & ILLUSTRATORS

Find cool websites and more books like this
one at www.facthound.com. Just type in the
book ID, and you're ready to go!

Book ID: 9781496543073